LETTERS HOME from MEXICO

Marcia S. Gresko

BLACKBIRCH PRESS, INC.
WOODBRIDGE, CONNECTICUT

Published by Blackbirch Press, Inc.
260 Amity Road
Woodbridge, CT 06525

©1999 by Blackbirch Press, Inc.
First Edition

e-mail: staff@blackbirch.com
Web site: www.blackbirch.com

Printed in Singapore

10 9 8 7 6 5 4 3 2 1

All photographs ©Corel Corporation

Library of Congress Cataloging-in-Publication Data
Gresko, Marcia S.
    Mexico / Marcia S. Gresko—1st ed.
      p.   cm.—(Letters home from—)
    Summary: Describes some of the sights and experiences on a trip through Mexico, including visits to Mexico City, Oaxaca, Chichen Itza, and Baja California.
    ISBN 1-56711-402-4
    1. Mexico—Description and travel—Juvenile literature. 2. Gresko, Marcia S.—Journeys—Mexico—Juvenile literature. [1. Mexico—Description and travel.] I. Title II. Series.
F1216.5.G74 1999   99-24507
917.204'836—dc21   CIP
                                                                     AC

TABLE OF CONTENTS

Arrival in . . .

Mexico City

We arrived in Mexico after a short plane flight. We landed in Mexico City, the capital. It's located in the middle of the country, about halfway between the Gulf of Mexico and the Pacific Ocean.

More than 24 million people live in crowded Mexico City. That makes it the largest city in the world! It's also North America's oldest city—dating back almost 700 years.

Our tour guide told us the buildings on the Plaza of the Three Cultures are like a history lesson. They represent the three cultures whose traditions have blended to create modern Mexico. The ruins of an Aztec temple remind us of the contributions of the country's Indian peoples. There is also a church built by the Spanish who conquered and ruled the land for 300 years. Next to this, there are glass and concrete office buildings, proof of Mexico's modern ways.

Mexico City

History is everywhere in Mexico City.

The bright, modern subway station where we caught the train this morning was built around an ancient Aztec pyramid!

At the ruins of the Templo Mayor (Great Temple), our guide explained that the Aztec Indians built their capital here almost 700 years ago. They called it Tenochtitlán. According to legend, the Aztec gods told the people to settle where they saw an eagle perched on a cactus eating a snake. This is the scene in the center of Mexico's red, green, and white striped flag.

Ceremonial area of Templo Mayor

National Cathedral

Flag in front of the National Cathedral

Tacuba Street near Zocalo

Spanish explorers searching for treasure—led by Hernando Cortez—conquered the Aztecs more than 450 years ago. They destroyed Tenochtitlán and ruled Mexico for 300 years.

We toured the Spanish-built palaces, churches, and mansions around the Zocalo. The Zocalo is one of the largest public squares in the world.

On one side of the square is the National Palace. It stands on the old palace grounds of the last Aztec king! Mexico's president and other top government leaders work there.

On another side is the National Cathedral. It has 14 chapels. Religion—mostly Catholicism—is an important part of Mexican life. The white stripe in the center of the Mexican flag stands for religion.

Mexico City

Mexico City's people proudly refer to the capital city simply as "Mexico." That's because it's the country's center of culture, business, and industry. When we left our hotel for the market, people were hurrying to their jobs in banks, offices, and shops. Trolleys, buses, and cars jammed the streets. One in four Mexicans lives and works in Mexico City. Successful middle-class Mexican families live in comfortable homes or apartments that have modern appliances like microwaves and VCRs. They shop in air-conditioned malls and go to modern schools.

Chilies

Mangos

Mexican currency

Herbal medicines

Stall with traditional sweets

Afternoon traffic

Our guide said that many other people are not so lucky. The city has grown so fast that there are many problems. There are not enough houses. Many people live in slums without running water or electricity. Air pollution is also a very serious problem.

At the market we saw stalls piled high with fruits, vegetables, and herbs. The climate in central Mexico makes it one of the best farming areas in the country. About one in three Mexicans still makes a living by farming. Mexican cooking uses many fruits and vegetables that taste great! I love mangos!

But the best thing at the market was a cool, tasty, blended fruit juice drink called a liquado!

Mexico City–Culture

On Sunday we did what many of the city's families were doing. We took a picnic and went to beautiful, bustling Chapultepec Park!

The enormous park was once the hunting grounds of Aztec kings. Now there are picnic grounds, lakes, an amusement park, a zoo, and really cool museums.

At the round, glass Museum of Modern Art we saw works by many of Mexico's most famous painters, such as Frida Kahlo. Mexican artists are famous for their murals, or wall paintings. Some of the most famous modern muralists are Diego Rivera, Jose Clemente Orozco, and David Alfaro Siqueiros. Their bold scenes show the history and struggles of the Mexican people.

Ballet Folklorico de Mexico

Ballet Folklorico de Mexico

Palace of
Fine Arts

Museum of
Modern Art

Frida Kahlo's
studio

After a filling lunch, we relaxed and listened to the lively music of a strolling mariachi band. These musicians play violins, guitars, and horns and dress in colorful outfits with wide-brimmed hats.

At night we visited the magnificent Palace of Fine Arts for a performance of the famous Ballet Folklorico. Dance is an important part of Mexican culture. Different regions have their own special music, costumes, and stories. But everyone liked the Mexican Hat Dance, the country's national dance!

Aztecs

Today, we took a day trip to the ruins of the city of Teotihuacán. Northeast of Mexico City, Teotihuacán was actually built before the Aztecs, but our guide said exploring it would help us understand them. The Aztecs were Mexico's last and most powerful Indian civilization.

The Aztecs believed in many gods. They built huge pyramids topped with temples to worship the gods. The main Aztec god was Huitzilopochtli, the god of war. The Aztecs waged war to capture prisoners to sacrifice to their gods. Human sacrifice was the most important part of the Aztec religion. They believed their gods needed human hearts and blood to survive (I'm glad I wasn't there for that!).

Pyramid of the Sun

Avenue of the Dead, Teotihuacán

Aztec carving

Pyramid of the Moon

Most Aztecs were farmers. The best things they grew were cacao trees. Inside cacao pods are the beans used to make chocolate! The Aztec emperor Montezuma supposedly loved chocolate so much, he had his servants make him 50 cups a day! The Aztecs' main food was a thin cornmeal pancake used to scoop up or wrap around other foods. The Spanish called it a tortilla.

The Aztecs were big on learning. They were the area's only early people to have schools. Inside a pyramid at Teotihuacán was a magnificent temple to Quetzalcóatl, the feathered serpent. He was worshipped by the Aztecs as the god of learning.

Aztecs

From Mexico City we traveled southeast about 340 miles to Oaxaca City. That's the capital of the state of Oaxaca. We went to explore the ruins of Monte Alban, and to see the exciting summer festival of Guelaguetza.

I read in my guidebook that the Aztecs were great storytellers and writers of poetry. They wrote stories and kept records using pictograms, or picture writing.

Though they were a warrior people, the Aztecs also had a tradition of arts and crafts. Religious services included dance and the music of drums, flutes, gongs, and rattles. Colorful featherwork was used to make banners,

Ancient ball court at Monte Alban

cloaks, headdresses, and other clothing. Pottery, weaving, woodcarving, and jewelry-making were other important crafts.

The Aztecs played games, too. One important ball game was part of religious ceremonies. The game was played on an enormous grass court. Players moved the ball around the court using only their hips and elbows. The stakes were high—losers could be sacrificed!

The Aztecs also studied the stars and had a calendar based on the Sun. They had a religious calendar that their priests used to figure out the best days for activities such as planting crops, going to war, and holding human sacrifices.

15

Oaxaca and Puerto Escondido

Saturday is the best day of the whole week in the city of Oaxaca! It's market day, and the city has the largest and best Indian market in Mexico. That's because the state has the largest population of native peoples in the country. More than 50 different Indian peoples live in Mexico. But the majority of Mexico's population is Mestizo, a mixture of European and Indian. The market was a maze of people. Stalls overflowed with tropical fruits and vegetables, meat, fish, and cheese. We bargained for one of Oaxaca's

Colorful glazed pottery

Fruit & vegetable vendors

Playa, Puerto Escondido

Boy with fish and tackle

famous pottery bowls. Our guide explained that markets like these have been going on for thousands of years.

Monday's harvest festival of Guelaguetza was even more exciting than market day! Festivals, or fiestas, are an exciting part of Mexican culture! There were traditional dances, food, and parades.

After all the excitement, it was great to take a day trip to quiet Puerto Escondido. It's about 200 miles south of Oaxaca. The town has lovely swimming beaches and one of the four best surfing beaches in the world. Giant waves curl in on themselves and form tunnels called "pipelines." It's so cool to watch surfers ride all the way through them!

The Yucatan Peninsula

From Oaxaca we flew about 570 miles northeast to the city of Merida. It's a 450-year-old Spanish city. From there we explored ancient Mayan Indian ruins in Uxmal and Chichen Itza. The Maya Indians flourished here for more than 1,000 years.

Modern Mayan boys

Mayan man in the Yucatan, Mexico

Palace, seventh-century Mayan ruins, Palenque

Merida is located in the Yucatan Peninsula in eastern Mexico. The peninsula is made up of three Mexican states, the country of Belize, and part of Guatemala. It sticks way out into the Gulf of Mexico.

The Yucatan is like a country inside a country. Most of Mexico's landscape is a mix of mountains and valleys, but the Yucatan is a huge, flat limestone plain. Large areas are covered by thick jungles where jaguars, monkeys, and colorful birds live. In these jungles, ancient Mayan cities lay hidden.

Today only 10% of the country's population lives here. Many people work on collective farms, called ejidos, growing corn, beans, and chilies. Henequen, used since ancient times to make rope, is still a major crop.

The Maya

Over the loudspeaker on the bus this morning, our guide told us about the Mayan civilization. The Maya were farming people who grew mostly beans, corn, squash, and cacao trees (chocolate—yum!). They also fished and hunted, gathered edible plants, and raised honeybees. Mayan farm families lived in plain, wooden homes with thatched roofs.

Mayan cities were the centers of Mayan life and culture. They were built to honor the many gods they believed in.

Uxmal was an important Mayan city for hundreds of years. Its beautiful stone and cement buildings are decorated with fancy cut stone mosaics. They have

Rattlesnake sculpture on Nunnery, Uxmal

Pyramid of the Magician, Uxmal

Human head in serpent form, AD 1000, Uxmal

masks of a rain god named Chac, turtles, and double-headed serpents. One of the most highly decorated buildings was called "The Nunnery" by the Spanish. It was an ancient learning center where Mayan leaders gathered to study and share information about the arts, science, and religion.

The Pyramid of the Magician was awesome! The guidebook said it was built over a period of 300 years, but the legend says it was built by a dwarf and a magician in just one night. Near the top was a throne shaped like a huge monster mask where Uxmal's rulers were probably crowned.

The Maya and Chichen Itza

We learned more about the powerful Maya at the ruins of their ancient city of Chichen Itza. That's about 75 miles east of Uxmal. Archeologists believe that the city was occupied by both the Maya and a later people, the Toltecs. Chichen Itza was the capital of the Yucatan Peninsula for about 200 years. Chichen Itza means "Place of the Well of the Itza." A deep, natural well was supposedly nearby. Mayan priests threw people and valuable objects into the sacred well to please the gods who lived there. Human sacrifice was an important part of the Mayan religion. The hearts of human sacrifices were placed in bowls held by the Chacmool statues. You can see these statues all around the temple ruins.

Temple of the Jaguars, Chichen Itza

El Caracol

Chacmool statue

South of the sacred well was a ball court and three huge temples. It was hard to believe that the Maya built them using only simple tools of flint and wood! Their stone walls, columns, and stairways were carved with figures of eagles, jaguars, warriors, skulls, and feathered serpents.

My favorite building was an observatory nick-named El Caracol, or "the snail." From there, skilled Mayan astronomers measured the movements of the Sun, Moon, and stars. They developed an accurate calendar and could even predict eclipses!

Acapulco and Puerto Vallarta

After exploring many of Mexico's beautiful ancient sights, it was time to enjoy some of the beautiful new sights. Some of the most popular beach resorts in the world are located on Mexico's southern Pacific coast. Here the weather is dreamlike—sunny and warm almost all year round.

Acapulco is Mexico's oldest resort city. The city was an important Spanish port for 250 years. Spanish ships sailed from Acapulco loaded with silver that was used to trade with Asia for silk, porcelain, spices, and ivory. Some of these valuable ships never made it to Asia. They were often raided by pirates!

Acapulco cliff diver climbing

Cliff, water, and diver, Acapulco

Fishermen returning,
Puerto Vallarta

Malecon,
Puerto Vallarta

Now cruise ships and more than 3 million tourists like us visit the city each year. The most awesome sights were the cliff divers who plunge more than 150 feet into the Pacific Ocean. They must time their dives just as a wave comes in or they will crash onto the sharp rocks below!

We went to another popular beach area, called Puerto Vallarta. It's about 400 miles northwest of Acapulco. It has excellent beaches and plenty of shopping in its cobblestone Old Town. One night we watched the sunset from the Malecon, the waterfront avenue overlooking the sparkling blue bay. Right then, I felt like I'd never want to come home.

Baja

Hola (hello) from California! Actually, we're in Baja California. The word baja means "lower" in Spanish. (Check a map and you'll see that Baja California is part of Mexico, not the United States.)

The Baja Peninsula looks like a long, skinny finger pointing south into the Pacific Ocean. It is about 800 miles long and ranges between 30 and 150 miles wide. The area is mostly hot and dry, with desert coastlines. On the west coast is the Pacific Ocean. On the east coast is the Sea of Cortes, also called the Gulf of California. The 150-mile-wide Sea of Cortes separates the

Zihuanatanejo sunset,
Pacific coast

Fishing boats, Puerto Angel Pacific coast

Mexican children holding lizards

peninsula from mainland Mexico. We took the long ferry ride across to get to La Paz, the capital of Baja South.

The Baja Peninsula is divided into two states—Baja California Norte (North) and Baja California Sur (South).

Baja North borders the United States. Its population is about seven times as large as Baja South. More people live in its city of Tijuana than in all of the rest of the Baja Peninsula combined! Most people in Baja North make their living in tourism. That means they depend on all the visitors like me to come and see cool stuff and spend lots of money!

Baja South

Our guide told us that if we wanted to explore lonely Baja South 30 years ago we would have done it by boat! The area only became a state in 1974.

Like the rest of the peninsula, Baja South is mostly hilly or mountainous desert. Many kinds of cacti grow in the hot, dry climate. We saw one kind, the giant cardon cactus. It was 60 feet high! It only grows in the Baja desert.

Really cool animals—like the desert tortoise, gila monster, big horn sheep, and puma—are all running around here.

Crashing waves, Playa Cerritos, Baja South

Cardon cactus, Baja South

Farmer fertilizing crops, Todos Santos

Cholla cactus

One of the largest animals in the world also makes Baja South its home, though only during the winter. From January through March, thousands of enormous gray whales swim 6,000 miles from their home in the waters off Alaska to several spots along the coast. In the warm waters here they give birth to their calves.

Tomorrow we'll travel even further south to Cabo San Lucas, at the tip of Baja South, where we're spending our last few days in Mexico.

Cabo San Lucas

It's hard to believe that Cabo San Lucas was once a poor fishing town with dusty dirt streets and smelly factories for canning fish! Now it's one of the most popular beach vacation spots in Mexico.

People come to sunbathe on the beautiful, white sand beaches. They also swim, snorkel, and scuba dive in the warm, clear waters. Serious fishers wrestle huge marlin and sailfish from the ocean off the Pacific coast. There are more than 800 species of fish in the area's waters!

Land's End,
Cabo San Lucas

Land's End,
Cabo San Lucas

My favorite spot was Land's End. It's at the very tip of the Baja Peninsula where the desert, rocks, and sea all come together. Here, Playa de Amor faces the peaceful Sea of Cortes and the pounding Pacific Ocean at the same time. A mysterious natural rock bridge called El Arco (The Arch) stands guard as sea lions and pelicans lounge in the sun. Our guide said that pirates once hid in nearby caves. When they spotted a treasure ship from Asia heading east to the port at Acapulco, they'd attack!

31

Glossary

Civilization an advanced stage of human organization, technology, and culture.

Climate the usual weather in a place.

Culture the way of life, including ideas, traditions, and customs, of a group of people.

Flourish to grow and succeed.

Mosaic a pattern or picture made up of pieces of colored glass, tile, or stones.

Native someone born in a particular place.

Ruins the remains of something that had collapsed or been destroyed.

Sacrifice to give something up for a good reason.

Slums overcrowded, poor, and neglected area of housing in a town or city.

Square an open area in a city or town, often used as a park, that is surrounded by streets on all four sides.

For More Information

Books

Berg, Elizabeth. *Mexico* (Festivals of the World). Milwaukee, WI: Gareth Stevens, 1997.

Harvey, Miles. *Look What Came From Mexico* (Look What Came From). Danbury, CT: Franklin Watts, Inc., 1998.

Parker, Edward A. *Mexico* (Country Insights). Chatham, NJ: Raintree/Steck Vaughn, 1998.

Staub, Frank J. *The Children of Sierra Madre* (World's Children). Minneapolis, MN: Carolrhoda Books, 1996.

Web Site
Virtual Palenque

Tour the ancient Mayan ruins in Mexico with a virtual tour guide who gives interesting facts—www.qvision.com/palenque/credits.htm.

Index